The Little Black Dog has PUPPIES

by J. B. SPOONER

Illustrations by

TERRE LAMB SEELEY

ARCADE PUBLISHING • NEW YORK

Many thanks to the Douglas and Kerr families

Arcade Publishing books may be purchased in bulk at special discounts for sales promotion, corporate gifts, fund-raising, or educational purposes. Special editions can also be created to specifications. For details, contact the Special Sales Department, Arcade Publishing, 307 West 36th Street, 11th Floor, New York, NY 10018 or info@skyhorsepublishing.com.

Arcade Publishing® is a registered trademark of Skyhorse Publishing, Inc.®, a Delaware corporation.

Visit our website at www.arcadepub.com.

10 9 8 7 6 5 4 3 2

Library of Congress Cataloging-in-Publication Data is available on file.

ISBN: 978-1-61145-006-4

Printed in China

DEDICATION

To Isabella ... and my litter of grandchildren yet to come
—J. B. Spooner

To my six kids ... Andrew, Barea, Jeremy, Molly, Harrison, and Samantha
—Terre Lamb Seeley

The little black dog had grown from a curious puppy to an outgoing, friendly young dog. She and her playmates, Grace Duffy, Abigail, Brandy, Shadrack, and Pasha, spent many hours romping on the beach and tirelessly fetching sticks from the water.

As summer wound down and fall settled in, the Captain began to notice some changes in his best friend.

"She's getting a bit thick about the middle," he explained to the vet when he called to schedule her for a check up.

The vet examined her and his suspicions were confirmed.

"Congratulations," he announced, "she's going to have her first litter of pups."

The Captain couldn't hide his delight.

"Well, my little mama dog," he said happily as he carried her back to the truck, "we'll have to make sure you eat two good meals a day and get plenty of exercise."

The little black dog went about her business as usual. Every morning she joined the Captain for an early walk along the beach. And every afternoon she made her regular rounds about town, always proudly bringing something home to the Captain.

a lost mitten ...

It might be a hat ...

or just a single, large oak leaf.

or an old shoe

Until one day ...

... one cold, rainy day ... the little black dog came home with a very big, but also a very little, surprise.

She was carefully carrying a tiny orange kitten in her mouth. The baby kitten was wet and shivering with a scraggly coat of matted fur.

The Captain remembered when the little black dog first came to him as an orphaned pup, cold, wet, and hungry. And just as he had done then, he set out a platter of milk … and he and his little black dog watched while the wobbly kitten lapped it up.

Then, to the Captain's surprise, his soon-to-be mama dog licked the stray kitten all over until she was clean and shiny.

"She must be practicing for when she has her pups," thought the Captain as he watched her carry the little kitten up the long flight of stairs.

She brought her to the spare bedroom and curled up around her on the big, empty bed. "Looks like I've lost my bunk mate," said the Captain to himself with a smile.

But by morning the little black dog was sprawled out in her usual spot at the foot of the Captain's bed.

Then one morning, to the Captain's surprise, his little black dog was not there. He looked in the spare room ... she wasn't there.

He called for her and whistled, but she didn't come.

The kitchen door was open. He knew she had gone somewhere in the middle of the night to have her pups ... but where? It had been a cold and rainy night, not good weather for having pups outside.

The Captain searched all day. He saw Pasha, the dog next door, down by the boathouse, but his little black dog was nowhere to be found. It was getting dark and the Captain was getting worried. It was too cold for newborn pups to be out all night.

He called the dog officer, but no one had seen her.

There was nothing he could do but wait, and he lay in bed listening for her. She had been born on a cold and rainy night and he hoped she knew how to take care of herself.

Early the next morning the Captain woke with a start. He heard the sound of scratching on the kitchen door and he hurried down the stairs to open it.

There was his little black dog, tired and hungry, wagging her tail at the sight of the Captain.

He made her a big breakfast, wishing he could ask her about her pups.

While the hungry little black dog lapped up every last bit of food, the Captain went to phone the dog officer to tell him she had returned.

When he came back to the kitchen, the door was open and the little black dog was gone. He ran outside and called for her, but he was too late. Again she was nowhere to be seen. "She couldn't have gone very far," he thought.

He looked all around the yard, under every shed,

and inside any possible hiding place, but he had no luck.

Again he saw Pasha down by the boathouse, but no sign of his little black dog. He would just have to wait for her to come home.

Finally that evening, after dark, the little black dog reappeared. She looked tired and wet from the rain. The Captain wrapped her in a towel and fed her by the fire, but this time he did not leave her side.

He knew she was protecting her pups by hiding them somewhere, and he was afraid they were not strong enough for the bitter cold nights.

When she lay down to take her usual after dinner nap, the Captain sat beside her and pretended to sleep as well.

Soon, just as he expected, the little black dog got up and headed for the door. The Captain waited while she opened the door, not wanting to reveal his plan. Then he quickly followed her, grabbing his flashlight on the way out.

He saw her turn the corner of the house. She was heading down the hill toward the beach.

The Captain traced her steps, careful not to make a sound. She was blacker than the night, making her way down the path to the boathouse.

Once on the beach, the little black dog disappeared. The Captain stopped beside the boathouse and looked around, shining his light in all the bushes. She was nowhere to be seen.

Then he saw Pasha moving quietly in the shadows. The Captain quickly followed Pasha's tracks in the sand.

There, around the corner of the building, was Pasha, sitting next to a small tunnel leading under the boathouse.

The Captain knelt down and shined his light into the tunnel. There was his little black dog curled up around a mound of black puppies ... busy licking each one in turn.

The Captain reached under and patted his little friend. Then he slowly moved his hand over her cozy pile of pups. They felt warm and dry in their sandy nest and the Captain was proud of how cleverly she had sheltered them from the wind and rain.

The little black dog was content to let the Captain take each pup, one by one, out from under the boathouse. He counted them out loud as he tucked them inside his shirt.

"One, two, three, four, five," his voice grew more and more excited, "six, seven, EIGHT, NINE! NINE PUPPIES! I can't believe it!" exclaimed the Captain in amazement, staring at the bundle of pups, each one as black and as perfect as the next.

"What a good mama dog you are," he said in awe of her accomplishment. "And a good watch dog you are too, Pasha! Come on, Mama, let's take them home." And he held the armful of pups close against his chest as he followed his little black dog back up to the house.

The Captain settled his new family in the "loony bin," which was a small pantry in the kitchen where the Captain had once nursed an oil soaked loon back to health.
He named each pup and noted their names and date of birth on the loony bin wall.

And as the little black puppies grew bigger and bigger, they could be seen every morning following the little black dog and the Captain on their daily walk down the beach ... each pup displaying a distinct white spot on one foot ... the unique markings of a new and special island breed known as the Vineyard Whitefoot.

1 DEC 1973

BLACK DOG PUPPED UNDER
THE BOATHOUSE NINE TIMES

THEY CAME TO BE KNOWN AS

BIG BOY	ANDRE
HONEY	TOBY HALL
BAGHEERA	KELLEY'S WELDER
BLOOD HOUND	PATTY
BUFFALOE	
(MIKE)	MRS SPOONER
	JOYCE'S AUNT
BIG GIRL	BILL HOLT
LITTLE GIRL	DON PARENT'S SON
THOR	HARRIS
SHASTA	SEELEY